The Oleander Press Ltd
16 Orchard Street
Cambridge CB1 1JT
England

www.oleanderpress.co.uk

For James and Seb

Two
by
Two

Many many years ago...
The world was big and bad.
God looked down from Heaven
And his people made him sad.
The world he'd made with light and love
Grew darker with each day.
He decided then to 'clean it up'
And wash the bad away.

"I know," said God, "I'll send a storm,
To fill the world with rain;
Get rid of everything I've made,
So I can start again."
He realised he would need some help
As he thought right through his plan.
He needed someone he could trust...
And Noah was the man.

God told him he must build an Ark
"To float on stormy seas."
So that, when the rain destroyed the land,
He could save his family.
"It must be big and made from wood
And three great stories high."
"Good grief!" cried Noah, looking up,
"Its roof will touch the sky!"

"It must be BIG." said God again,
"As it won't just carry you."
"Well, apart from the wife and kids..."
Noah asked God, "...who?"
"Why, all my creatures," He explained,
"From the jungle to the sky;
Two of each must board the Ark
So that they can multiply."

For seven days and seven nights
Noah laboured on the Ark,
And when the last nail was hammered in,
He saw the sky was dark.
He started loading the animals,
Seven by seven and two by two.
"Thousands of creatures!" Noah cried,
"My Ark's a floating ZOO!"

There was every type of animal
You could ever hope to find.
Birds and reptiles, insects too,
Of each and every kind.
Grinning, snapping crocodiles;
Fuzzy, buzzing bees;
Pink, pot-bellied pigs followed
Porcupines with fleas.

Tiny, pink-eyed mice
Gazed up at tall giraffes,
While funny orange orangutans
Made hyenas laugh!
Spotty, dotty leopards
Chased zebras – white, with stripes;
Snuffly, gruffly wildebeest
Complained the skunks smelled ripe!

Lumbering, bumbling elephants
Ridden by squawking parrots;
Twin hopping, hungry rabbits
Had come in hope of carrots.
Slippery, scaly snakes
Slid after warty frogs
And pure white snowy owls
Swooped over cats and dogs.

Noah watched the animals
As they trundled on in twos.
He made his way up to the Ark
As they slithered, crawled and flew.
"All aboard! All aboard!"
Noah checked there were no more.
"Ready to sail!" he said to God,
Then safely shut the door.

As the stormy sky turned black
And thunder rolled on by,
A fork of lightning speared the clouds
And brightened up the sky.
Drip, drip drip – the rain came down,
And then began to pour;
The ground was one big puddle
As the drops fell more and more.

The water got deep; then deeper!
The Ark began to float.
With all his passengers safely on board
Noah thanked God for their boat.
The rain lashed down from Heaven,
As heavy as could be,
Destroying all that God had made
As the land joined with the sea.

For forty days and forty nights
The rain just didn't stop.
The whole world now was ocean
With just the Ark on top.
Inside the Ark, all safe and dry,
The animals had all been fed.
Noah made sure that all was well
Before he went to bed.

Taking a walk out on deck
He looked up and saw the moon ~
The clouds had gone and the rain had stopped!
He hoped they'd see land soon.
The next few weeks were sunny and warm
With not a cloud in the sky;
So Noah released a bright white dove
Saying, "Go little one – you must fly."

But when the dove returned to him
As no resting place was found,
He knew the sea was still too high ~
Its waters still covered the ground.
After one more week of waiting,
The dove flew again through the sky.
When it returned with an olive leaf,
Noah knew some ground was dry.

He said, "I'll send it one last time,
To find a place to rest.
We'll know if it doesn't return to me
It's busy building a nest."
So, when the dove did not return,
He knew they were home and dry;
And on swinging open the doors of the Ark
He saw a rainbow painting the sky.

God said, "This is my promise ~
I shall still send rain;
But only enough to make the earth grow,
I'll never destroy it again.
Well done my dear Noah," He praised,
"For keeping my animals dry.
Now you must let them out of the Ark
To go forth and multiply."

Noah did as God decreed
And the creatures poured onto the land.
They ran to make homes in the jungles,
The swamps, the trees and the sands.
Noah and his happy family
Stretched and blinked in the sun.
It was time for them to leave the Ark,
Now that His work was done.

Noah looked forward to building a home
In a world that was shiny and new;
But one thing he would never forget
Was his time in the 'floating zoo'.

WHY NOT DRAW YOUR FAVOURITE
ANIMALS FROM THE STORY ON
THESE PAGES?

BE SURE TO CHECK OUT THE
OTHER FABULOUS CHILDREN'S
STORIES AT

WWW.OLEANDERPRESS.COM

Photo © Helen Watson-Jones

Born in Northamptonshire in 1974, Leanne Kilpatrick has colourful memories of celebrating religious holidays with her vast extended family. With Christianity playing a large part in her own childhood, she firmly believes that children today can benefit from a basic understanding of its teachings.

In re-writing a collection of much loved bible stories to rhyme, Leanne hopes to convey their moral message and to bring them vividly to life in the imagination of the young reader or listener.
'Two By Two' is Leanne's first children's book – being perhaps inspired by her life at home in rural Warwickshire where she lives with her husband Eric, sons James and Sebastian, and a menagerie of dogs, chickens, ducks and guinea fowl.

Her royalties will be donated to UNICEF.

Printed in Great Britain
by Amazon

86244509R00016